Ye olde book
belongeth to...

_____

_____

_____

The Knight Who Might
An original concept by author Lou Treleaven
© Lou Treleaven
Illustrated by Kyle Beckett

MAVERICK ARTS PUBLISHING LTD
Studio 11, City Business Centre, 6 Brighton Road, Horsham,
West Sussex, RH13 5BB, +44 (0)1403 256941
© Maverick Arts Publishing Limited
Published August 2020

A CIP catalogue record for this book
is available at the British Library.

ISBN 978-1-84886-483-2

Maverick
publishing

www.maverickbooks.co.uk

To all of us who dream - L.T.
For Lauren - K.B.

The Knight Who Might

Written by **Lou Treleaven**

Ilustrated by **Kyle Beckett**

In a tower on a hill lived **The Knight Who Might.**

He tried really hard to be a **knight**. He tried with all his **might**.

He tried really hard to ride a horse.
He clung on and closed his eyes.

"One day, I might be a knight," he said, as he rode his horse up the hill and into the sunset. Where he fell off.

"Oof!"

"You might not," said the horse.
(It was a magic horse.)
"But I might," said the knight.

He tried really hard to use a sword. He **swished** and **swiped**. "One day, I might be a knight," he said, as he accidentally drove his sword into a tree and couldn't get it out.

"You might not," said the sword.
(It was a magic sword.)
"But I might," said the knight.

He tried really hard to wear his armour.
He **clinked**, **clanked** and **clonked**.
"One day, I might be a knight," he said, as he put his helmet on backwards and fell in a muddy puddle.

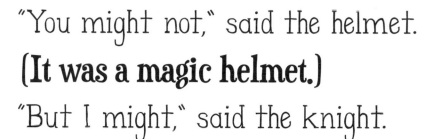

"You might not," said the helmet.
(It was a magic helmet.)
"But I might," said the knight.

"I know!" said **The Knight Who Might.** "I will enter this competition for knights. Someone has to win, and I might."

Knights
Wanted
for ye Olde
Tournament

"He'll **lose**," said the horse.

"You've got a **point**," said the sword.

"He's **heading for disaster**," said the helmet.
"Let's hide. He can't be a knight without us."

The Knight Who Might called for his faithful horse. He searched for his trusty sword. He hunted for his lucky helmet. They weren't there.

"I may not have the things a knight needs, but I might be a knight. I just might!" said the knight, and he began the long journey alone.

"He'll be **exhausted**," said the horse.

"He'll be **cut** to pieces," said the sword.

"He'll lose his **head**," said the helmet.

They looked at each other.
"Jump on my back," said the horse.
"And **hurry!**"

When they arrived, they found **The Knight Who Might** getting ready to fight **The Lord With the Scary Looking Sword.**

"I can't do it," said the knight. "For the first time in my life,
I'm **The Knight Who Might Not.**"

"Don't say that. **We can do it**," said the horse,
nudging him onto her back.

"Yes, **cut it out**," said the sword,
jumping into his hand.

"**Heading for victory!**" said the helmet, hurling itself onto his head.

And together they charged towards
The Lord With the Scary Looking Sword.

Closer and **closer** they galloped.

"We might do it! We just might!" cried the knight.

"You're right!" cheered the horse, the sword and the helmet.

"We **really** might!"

Closer and **closer**
they galloped, until...

The Knight Who Might was knocked senseless to the ground.

But when he had recovered and had a cup of tea and a biscuit, the judges announced: "The prize for **outstanding bravery** in the **face of certain defeat** goes to...

...The Knight Who Might!"

"**We did it!**" cheered the knight.

And he picked up his **trusty** sword,
put on his **lucky** helmet, and rode his
faithful horse up the hill and into the sunset...